OLLIE'S STORY: AN AMISH HEALING REDUX

A SHORT STORY

BETH WISEMAN

To my beloved fur babies—Rocky and Adrian

ACCLAIM FOR BOOKS BY BETH
WISEMAN

The House That Love Built

"This sweet story with a hint of mystery is touching and emotional. Humor sprinkled throughout balances the occasional seriousness. The development of the love story is paced perfectly so that the reader gets a real sense of the characters." ~ ROMANTIC TIMES, 4-STAR REVIEW

"[The House That Love Built] is a warm, sweet tale of faith renewed and families restored." ~ BOOKPAGE

Need You Now

"Wiseman, best known for her series of Amish novels, branches out into a wider world in this story of family, dependence, faith, and small-town Texas, offering a character for every reader to relate to . . . With an enjoyable cast of outside characters, *Need You Now* breaks the molds of small-town stereotypes. With issues ranging from special education and teen cutting to what makes a marriage strong, this is a compelling and worthy read." ~ BOOKLIST

"Wiseman gets to the heart of marriage and family interests in a way that will resonate with readers, with an intricately written plot featuring elements that seem to be ripped from current headlines. God provides hope for Wiseman's characters even in the most desperate situations." ~ ROMANTIC TIMES, 4-STAR REVIEW

"You may think you are familiar with Beth's wonderful story-telling gift but this is something new! This is a story that will stay with you for a long, long time. It's a story of hope when life seems hopeless. It's a story of how God can redeem the seemingly unredeemable. It's a message the Church, the world needs to hear." ~ SHEILA WALSH, AUTHOR OF *GOD LOVES BROKEN PEOPLE*

"Beth Wiseman tackles these difficult subjects with courage and grace. She reminds us that true healing can only come by being vulnerable and honest before our God who loves us more than anything." ~ DEBORAH BEDFORD, BESTSELLING AUTHOR OF *HIS OTHER WIFE, A ROSE BY THE DOOR, AND THE PENNY* (COAUTHORED WITH JOYCE MEYER)

The Land of Canaan Novels

"Wiseman's voice is consistently compassionate and her words flow smoothly." ~ PUBLISHERS WEEKLY REVIEW OF *SEEK ME WITH ALL YOUR HEART*

"Wiseman's third Land of Canaan novel overflows with romance, broken promises, a modern knight in shining armor and hope at the end of the rainbow." ~ ROMANTIC TIMES

"In *Seek Me with All Your Heart*, Beth Wiseman offers readers a heart-warming story filled with complex characters and deep emotion. I instantly loved Emily, and eagerly turned each page, anxious to learn more about her past—and what future the Lord had in store for her." ~ SHELLEY SHEPARD GRAY, BESTSELLING AUTHOR OF *THE SEASONS OF SUGARCREEK SERIES*

"Wiseman has done it again! Beautifully compelling, *Seek Me with All Your Heart* is a heart-warming story of faith, family, and renewal. Her characters and descriptions are captivating, bringing the story to life with the turn of every page." ~ AMY CLIPSTON, BESTSELLING AUTHOR OF *A GIFT OF GRACE*

The Daughters of the Promise Novels

"Well-defined characters and story make for an enjoyable read." ~ ROMANTIC TIMES REVIEW OF *PLAIN PURSUIT*

"A touching, heartwarming story. Wiseman does a particularly great job of dealing with shunning, a controversial Amish practice that seems cruel and unnecessary to outsiders . . . If you're a fan of Amish fiction, don't miss *Plain Pursuit!*" ~ KATHLEEN FULLER, AUTHOR OF *THE MIDDLEFIELD FAMILY NOVELS.*

ALSO BY BETH WISEMAN

Contemporary Women's Fiction
The House that Love Built
Need You Now
The Promise

Daughters of the Promise Series
Plain Perfect
Plain Pursuit
Plain Promise
Plain Paradise
Plain Proposal
Plain Peace

Land of Canaan Series
Seek Me With All Your Heart
The Wonder of Your Love
His Love Endures Forever

Amish Secrets Series

Her Brothers Keeper
Love Bears All Things
Home All Along

Amish Journeys Series
    Hearts in Harmony
    Listening to Love
    A Beautiful Arrangement

An Amish Inn Series
    A Picture of Love
    An Unlikely Match
    A Season of Change

An Amish Bookstore Series
    The Bookseller's Promise
    The Story of Love
    Hopefully Ever After

Stand-Alone Amish Novel
    The Amish Matchmakers

Short Stories/Novellas
    An Amish Adoption
    The Messenger
    Return of the Monarchs
    An Amish Christmas Gift
    An Amish Healing

Surf's Up Novellas
    A Tide Worth Turning

Message In A Bottle
The Shell Collector's Daughter
Christmas by the Sea

Collections
An Amish Christmas Bakery
An Amish Reunion
An Amish Homecoming
An Amish Spring
Amish Celebrations
An Amish Heirloom
An Amish Christmas Love
An Amish Home
An Amish Harvest
An Amish Year
An Amish Cradle
An Amish Second Christmas
An Amish Garden
An Amish Miracle
An Amish Kitchen
An Amish Wedding
An Amish Christmas
Healing Hearts
An Amish Love
An Amish Gathering
Summer Brides

Memoir
Writing About the Amish

GLOSSARY

- *ach*: oh
- *boppli*: baby
- *daed*: dad
- *danki*: thank you
- *Englisch/Englischer*: non-Amish person
- *Gott*: God
- *gut nacho*: good night
- *haus*: house
- *lieb/liebed*: love/loved
- *mei*: my
- *nee*: no
- *sohn*: son
- *wie bischt*: hello/how are you?
- *ya*: yes

CHAPTER 1

*W*here are my humans? And why do my paws, snout, and belly hurt?

Hank instinctively carried himself away from the biggest fire he'd ever seen in his short life. Orange glowing flames shot to the sky amid a billowing cloud of black smoke. It smelled like the gas Mr. Hoover had put in the car earlier—the vehicle that was taking them home to Montgomery, Indiana. They were returning from a vacation in Pennsylvania to visit Nellie and John's family.

Where are Nellie and John? They would know how to help Hank. They were the most loving pet owners alive. Even though he'd never lived with anyone else, Hank was sure of it.

As ice crunched beneath muddy paws that ached, Hank's belly hurt, but not the same crampy way as when he was hungry. This was different. In addition to the pain in his stomach, there was a burning sensation on his snout, and when he licked his parched lips, he tasted what he thought was blood.

Loud sirens were everywhere, with flashing blue and red lights and people rushing around all over the place. He'd never seen anything like this, and again, he wondered where Nellie and John were.

He huddled beneath a small tree at the far end of the ravine, away from the crowd, eying what used to be the car they'd traveled in. He shuddered as boom after boom lit up the sky, sending debris flying in all directions.

As he thought back, he recalled Nellie screaming, a loud and scary sound. Hank had closed his eyes from within the small carrier he'd been traveling in. He loved the enclosure filled with blankets and his favorite toys. He remembered a strange feeling, almost as if the vehicle was flying. It was only his second time to travel in a car. Normally, he rode with Nellie and John in a black buggy that was pulled by one of their horses.

His mind blurred, and even at his young age—ten months, he thought—he'd sensed impending doom. The pungent smells, the flying, the screaming . . .

Then, before he'd been able to grasp what was happening, it felt as if he was transported on a feathery cloud that landed him beneath the tree where he now sat, shivering and in pain.

As he tried to ignore the smoke, the fire, and the chaos, he forced himself to stand, flinching from the pain. His eyes scanned the people who were gathering around the ravine where the smoke was still heavy, but the fire was becoming smaller. Cars had pulled over along the two-lane highway. Women had their mouths covered with their hands. Most of the men shook their heads with drawn expressions on their faces. Some of them wore straw hats like the people Hank was used to being around. Others were in clothes that Nellie said the *Englishers* wore, bright colors and different styles. But almost everyone had on a coat, and as small icy pellets pounded against Hank's fur, he knew he had to find his way home. He'd heard John tell Nellie that they were close to home.

He'd also heard the man driving—Charles—say there was ice on the roads so he would have to slow down.

Hank began shivering so badly from the cold and the pain that was getting worse that he wanted to just lie down in the snow. But something inside nudged him to be strong. Nellie and John would want him to find his way home.

Trembling, he began his trek, on shaky legs, in the direction he thought would take him to his house. He thought his home was on the other side of the highway, and he had no idea how to cross the roadway without getting run over. But it was his only way to get home. Nellie and John would find a way to meet him there, then everything would be okay. Nellie would doctor him the way she had done when he'd stepped on a nail in the barn. It had hurt a lot and caused his foot to swell, and he had to eat pills mashed up in his food for a while. None of it had been pleasant, but Nellie's sweet voice and gentle care had left him knowing he would be okay.

Hank forced himself to walk. Each step felt like he was walking on pins and needles, the kind found in Nellie's sewing basket. He felt ice accumulating on his ears, and the blood on his nose felt like it was freezing.

He eyed the two-lane highway. Home was on the other side. It had to be.

3

When he'd finally inched closer to the roadway, cars flew by, splashing a wintry mix of ice and snow in his direction. He shook all over. A few of the automobiles, as he'd heard Nellie call the cars, slowed and stopped. Some people stepped out of them while others peered out their windows.

Hank knew that if he didn't try to run across the highway now, he might not ever be able to get to the other side where home was.

His paws ached as he made his way in front of a car that might have been green. He'd heard Nellie and John talk about colors, but he didn't think he saw the same colors as his owners.

The big dark-colored car slammed on the brakes, which reminded Hank of the way their driver must have hit the brakes before all the bad stuff happened. Hank braced for impact by instinctively laying on his belly even though the pain stabbed at his abdomen like a knife. He opened his eyes in time to see four wheels, two on each side, zoom by, delivering a whoosh of icy snow that filled his nostrils, making it hard for him to breathe.

He forced himself to stand on all four paws, searing pain in every step as he weaved his way through the traffic. Thoughts of a warm fire, Nellie's gentle touch, and his special spot on the recliner in the living room were all that kept him going.

Hank had the best owners, and they'd get him all fixed up.

He just had to find his way home.

CHAPTER 2

O ver the next few dizzying hours, time crawled slowly. Hank's paws ached, and his throat was so dry he found himself panting uncontrollably.

After crossing the highway, he was in the middle of a field, the kind of land where John turned grass into food for the cows to eat. Hank liked to lay on the back of the couch by the window and watch John guide the mules as he chopped the grass up and then rolled it into big bales. On pretty days, he loved to roll around in the freshly cut hay.

But the grass in this field was tall and icy, pricking Hank's paws and sides with each painful step. As his vision began to blur from the snow, he thought about giving up. There wasn't even any blood coming from his nose. It felt frozen in place, and Hank feared that Nellie and John might never find him out here in the overgrown field, frozen to death.

He laid down--panting, sore, and defeated--before he closed his eyes to succumb to whatever was happening.

But a loud voice in the icy wind bellowed for him to take a deep breath.

Maybe he'd dreamed it, but Hank lifted his head, sniffed the air, and smelled smoke. As he struggled to take breaths around the frozen blood on his nose and mouth, he recognized the welcoming aroma. It wasn't like the stinky smoke at the ravine. It was the woody smell of Nellie and John's fireplace, which meant he was close to home.

Just a little bit farther, he thought as he struggled to stand.

Hank wasn't sure if he could take one more step, but the feathery feel of something beneath his paws warmed not only the pads of his feet but his resolve. He had to make it home. Giving up wasn't an option if he wanted to see Nellie and John again, if he wanted the warmth of the fire, Nellie's gentle touch, and the feel of the soft cushion beneath him in his favorite recliner.

As he shuffled across the field, he forced himself to pick up speed, the pain piercing his paws now, but there was a white house in the distance. It wasn't Nellie and John's home. At least, he didn't think so. With everything blanketed in white, it was hard to tell. But a swirling cloud of gray smoke rose from a chimney like the one at Nellie and John's house.

Someone would help him. Hank just had to get there. He limped the final course to the stranger's house, but moved in an awkward, off-balanced pace to get there.

Hank eyed the porch steps covered in slick, icy snow. Four more steps, and he would be underneath the protection of a covered space. Hopefully, whoever lived there would find him and take him in.

He slid twice trying to paw his way up the slippery steps. Finally, he made it, found his way across the porch, and curled up behind a rocking chair. Hank wanted to bark and call for help, but when he tried to utter a sound, only a whimper escaped. He closed his eyes to rest as darkness began to fall.

HANK WASN'T sure how long he slept, but when he blinked his eyes open, the sun was shining. Half his body was in the shadow of the rocking chair, and he could feel the heat of the sun on part of his back.

Yawning was painful as he took in his surroundings, still shivering from the cold and unwilling to move. He ached from head to toe. Why hadn't anyone found him?

He ran his tongue along his bottom lip, which seemed to have scabbed from the blood on his snout.

This was a smaller house than John and Nellie's. The porch wasn't as long, and the barn was much closer than at his owners' house. But whoever lived here must be the same kind of people because a black buggy was on the other side of the fenced front yard. The white picket fence was like the one at his home, and there was a cleared stone pathway that led across the yard to the house. On either side, brownish hues of dry grass poked through the melting snow.

Hank longed to make his way down the steps and into

the yard. Despite his wounds, he had to "go potty" as Nellie called it. But when he tried to stand up, his paws wouldn't allow it, and a burning sensation on his underside caused him to fold into himself. He was tempted to put a paw across his face when he tinkled in place, but his snout was too sore to hide his shame. He was forced to lay in his own urine, worried that if he was found, no one would help him because he stunk. He couldn't remember when he'd eaten or drunk anything, so maybe he didn't smell as bad as he felt. His throat was dry, and he still didn't feel like he could bark.

He was startled when the screen door on the porch opened with a squeak. A woman stepped across the threshold carrying a basket and a box, then she closed the wooden door behind her. Hank's ears perked up at the smell of food, but when he tried again to bark, nothing came out. His heart ached when the woman began to move down the porch steps.

She wore a black overcoat and black bonnet, just like Nellie wore during the cold months. But this woman didn't look like Nellie, who had dark hair. This lady had strands of light-colored hair that escaped from her bonnet.

Hank tried to bark again, but only a small whimper escaped. All he could do was dream about the warmth inside the house and about Nellie and John eventually finding him.

Suddenly, the woman looked over her shoulder and backed up until she stood on the porch staring at Hank. Would she help him or shoo him away? He'd heard some people don't like dogs.

She moved slowly, placing her basket and box atop

one of the other three rocking chairs on the porch. After she moved toward him, she squatted down a couple of feet away. *"Wie bischt, mei* little friend."

Hank raised his head a little higher even though his snout screamed in opposition, aching all the while as he stuck out his tongue and panted, partially from fear but more so in anticipation of someone taking care of him.

The woman inched closer to him. *"Wie bischt,"* she repeated barely above a whisper. "Are you going to let me help you?"

Hank's insides warmed at the tenderness in her voice.

She offered Hank the topside of her hand like he'd seen other people do when they were first introduced to a furry friend. Hank sniffed her hand, and while she didn't look like Nellie, she smelled like Nellie. *Maybe lavender soap.*

The woman began to stroke Hank's back, and with each stroke, she drew back dirt and icy mud from his fur. Her actions were soothing, but his belly burned, and when he moved, he saw fresh blood, which caused him to tremble with fear more than pain. Maybe he was going to die after all.

She took back her hand, frowned, and studied him for a long while before she slipped both hands underneath him. *What's she doing?*

As she lifted Hank into her arms, he yelped. He was happy to have his voice back, but he'd caused the woman to jump, which wasn't his intention. Hank didn't want her to drop him or be afraid of him. He lowered his head into the nook of her arm, ashamed that he was getting icy dirt on her black coat, not to mention how he must smell.

The woman—he wished he knew her name—carried him into the house, and a blast of warm air hit him like welcomed sunshine after a bath. She took him straight to the bathroom, wrapped him in a towel, and then cradled him in her arms like humans cradle a baby. Hank felt safe even though he hurt all over.

Wait . . . no, no, no. She was heading back to the porch with him. *Please don't leave me in the cold to die.*

Still holding him, she retrieved her bag and box of whatever smelled so good from the porch and placed them on the kitchen table. Hank breathed a huge sigh of relief when they were back in the warm house.

After crossing through the living room, they entered a small room with a metal exam table. Hank had seen a room like this before, and he began to tremble again. He remembered getting shots and other unpleasantries that had occurred atop a table like this one.

The lady placed a clean white towel on the table before laying Hank down. The billowy towel began to absorb dirt and blood as his new caretaker began to inspect every inch of him. His trembling stilled. It was warm in the room, but he began to pant, and his breaths were becoming more labored. The woman was gentle with her touch, but Hank wasn't looking forward to being poked and prodded no matter how pretty the lady was, how soft her hands were, or how sweet her voice.

As she eased him onto his side, more blood oozed from his belly. He didn't want her touching that area. She leaned closer to him, her face near his, as she gently scratched the top of his head.

"*Ach, mei* friend, we need to stitch this up." The woman

flinched, causing a flurry of anxiety to rush over Hank. *Stitch this up? What does that mean?* "I'm sorry," she said, her face crinkled into an expression that worried Hank even more.

She reached for a bottle from a shelf against the wall, shook the contents into a small shallow bowl, and then offered it to Hank. He moved his head into a position where he could sniff the bowl. It wasn't water, but he began to lap up the liquid. He was so thirsty, and even though it tasted grainy and strange, he drank it all.

"There you go," she said, smiling now, and Hank's throat didn't feel as dry. *That wasn't so bad.* Then she reached for another bottle, cringing again, and Hank's stomach churned. "This will sting a bit."

Sting? He'd heard that word. Nellie had wrangled with a bee, and a sting was the result. It had brought tears to her eyes. *Wait . . . I don't want any stings.* But when the liquid met with his matted wound, Hank gave her a warning in the form of a nip on her arm. It wasn't meant to hurt her, just to let her know that whatever she poured on his belly was causing him pain.

Right away, he felt bad for snapping at her, and he was glad to see he hadn't broken the surface. Even though pain engulfed his tummy, he sensed she was trying to help him. But he wasn't interested in her getting near his belly.

She touched him where it hurt anyway, pressing a warm towel against the place where all the blood was coming from, and then she began to rub some thick and milky stuff all around the area, and it didn't feel good at all. But he didn't have the heart to snap at her again.

After she sprinkled more grainy droplets into a bowl

of warm water, she offered it to him, and Hank drank it all. Within seconds, his head began to spin, the room became blurry, and he could feel an odd sensation in his belly. Was she giving him those stitches she'd mentioned?

He wasn't sure. He felt pressure, but it didn't hurt. And he was starting not to care what she did as he began to yawn.

After a while, he felt awake but asleep, an odd feeling he wasn't familiar with, but he wasn't in nearly as much pain.

"There. You look like a new doggie," she said, smiling.

Hank smiled on the inside as the room spun.

"I have to leave you for a while to attend two funerals." Her smile vanished as she retrieved a kennel.

Hank fought the fogginess in his mind as she eased him into the cage. He didn't want to be confined. He wanted to be back in her arms, feeling safe like he did before.

Funerals? Who died? And where are Nellie and John?

CHAPTER 3

*W*hen Hank opened his eyes, it took him a few minutes to remember where he was. In a kennel atop the metal table. He felt clean and didn't smell badly anymore, but his belly was tight, tender, and covered with some sort of dressing. He also had something that felt like a bandage across his snout and another one by his left ear. *Gauze.* That's what he'd heard Nellie call it when she doctored John's arm once.

Where was the pretty lady with the soft voice and light-colored hair? He began to whimper, and the louder his whine became, the more his head hurt. How long could he survive in this kennel? Then, he saw a small platter of water in the far corner of what he feared might be his new home.

Laying almost sideways on his belly, in an awkward position to avoid the tenderness on his tummy, he began to drink. He felt a little better with each gulp, but he hoped he didn't sleep again. He needed to be alert and aware of his surroundings.

He wailed even louder between panting when he heard a door open somewhere in the house. Even though he tried to bark, only pitiful moans escaped, but he made as much noise as he could until he heard loud footsteps heading his way. His ears perked up when he saw it was the woman who had taken him in.

"You poor *boppli*." She unlatched the lever on the kennel and slowly reached a hand inside, gently stroking Hank's back, which seemed to be one of the few places where he didn't have a bandage. "I'm sorry I left you," she said.

Hank's panting began to slow down as the feel of the lady's gentle touch calmed him. He wanted to stand, though, so on shaky legs, he lifted himself to his feet.

"Will you let me hold you?" She patted the entrance of the kennel, and Hank shuffled slowly toward her, then he let her ease her arms beneath him. He stifled a yelp since she moved slowly and took care to maneuver around his wounds, eventually cradling him like a baby. Even though he was sore, he felt safe in her arms.

She moved out of the small room with the kennel and shelves and into the big room with the couch. "You're shivering." She laid him down on the couch before she hung her black cape and bonnet on the rack by the front door, and then she wriggled out of her boots.

Hank trembled, partly from the cold, but he was also apprehensive. Nothing was familiar. Where were Nellie and John? He missed his favorite recliner, but staying put on this new furniture didn't require much effort. And when was he going to get some food?

After the woman added a log to the glowing embers in

her fireplace, she sat on the couch and eased Hank into her arms.

He closed his eyes. If he were a cat, he'd be purring. He liked being in her arms.

She lowered her face to his, almost touching the bandage on his nose, and Hank decided that she deserved a big wet kiss.

"*Danki*," she said as she giggled before she began to rock him in her arms. Hank yawned.

"Do you think I'll ever see that man again?" She sighed, still cradling him like a baby. "I'm thinking I won't."

Hank didn't open his eyes, hoping she would keep talking. Maybe she would offer a clue about his owners. *What man? John?*

"If no one claims you, would you like to stay here?" She leaned down again and lowered her nose to Hank's snout without touching the bandage on his face. Hank attempted to nod, and the woman chuckled. "Then it's settled. And we need a name for you."

She was a nice lady, but . . . *I have a name. Hank. And my owners are John and Nellie.*

His new friend was startled when her phone rang in her purse. Hank shifted slightly as she reached for it on the coffee table.

He'd heard Nellie and others say that phones weren't allowed or were for emergencies. Hank assumed there must be a lot of emergencies because everyone around him had a phone.

The woman listened to the speaker, then laughed and said, "Lizzie . . . the man is grieving, and he lives in another state. I think your matchmaking skills might be put to better use somewhere else."

Hank's ears perked up. *Grieving?* He was pretty sure that was a type of sadness. But it was confusing since his new caregiver had laughed prior to the comment.

"*Nee*, Lizzie, I don't think I should come. We have more snow on the way." Hank's chest tightened as he wondered if he would be left in the kennel again. He lifted his eyes to hers, willing her to see how he felt inside. Could she see how scared he would be if she left him unattended?

She—again he wondered what her name was—listened for a few moments, then said, "I'm sure the family will return to settle Nellie and John's affairs. If it's *Gott's* plan for me to see Jeremiah again, then it will happen."

Jeremiah. That name sounded familiar, but he wasn't sure why. Hank tried to find his voice, to bark, to let this nice lady know that Nellie and John were his owners, but only a whimper escaped. Right away, the woman's hand found his special spot behind his good ear and rubbed. It felt so satisfying, but Hank's thoughts were scrambled like the leftover eggs Nellie fed him sometimes.

Where are Nellie and John? Someone needed to let them know that Hank was safe. And, as nice as this lady was, Hank missed his people, his chair, his home. *And who is Jeremiah?* he wondered again.

The woman listened to the other person talking for a while, then she stiffened all over and stopped rubbing Hank behind his ear.

"What do you mean that someone should have spoken at the funeral about the dog who perished in the accident?

I didn't know Nellie and John had a dog." The lady put a hand to her mouth and listened again. "Are you saying that Nellie and John took their dog on vacation to Pennsylvania with them?"

Yes! Yes! They took me with them to Pennsylvania, and we were almost home when we got separated. What accident? Were John and Nellie hurt?

The lady listened some more. Hank held his breath and strained to hear, but he couldn't.

"Did you say the dog was a Border Collie?" She looked down at Hank and blinked her eyes a few times. Her eyes glassed over with moisture.

The call ended, and she put the phone beside her on the couch before she stood up carrying Hank.

Please don't put me back in the kennel. I'm feeling confused. I miss Nellie and John. Hank had so many questions he wished he could verbalize so this woman could help him get home.

But she didn't go toward the room with the kennel. Instead, she pulled back a pretty cover on a big bed in another room and laid him down. After she put on her bedclothes and crawled under the covers, she reached over and rubbed Hank's back. He liked it when she did that, but he couldn't fully appreciate it with all these thoughts swirling around in his mind.

"You can't possibly be Nellie and John's dog." The lady sniffled. "That would be nothing short of a miracle."

Then I guess I'm a miracle. Hank's head hurt. So did his heart. *Please take me to Nellie and John. They must be really worried about me.*

CHAPTER 4

Ollie wasn't sure how much time had gone by, maybe seven or eight days. *Ollie*. That's what she had started calling him. He found his voice and barked for the first couple of days, hoping she would get the message. His name was Hank.

But Ollie was starting to grow on him, as was this lady. She even bought him a ball to play with outside when the weather was nice enough. He decided he would be Ollie until he was reunited with Nellie and John. Then he'd be back to Hank.

"Come on, Ollie, we need to get ready to go on a short trip." She stood from where she sat in a chair on the front porch, a blanket wrapped around her shoulders.

Ollie hopped through the white slush of melted snow with his new yellow tennis ball in his mouth. He dropped it at her feet just like she'd taught him to do. She leaned down, smiling, and scratched him behind the ears. He was in pretty good shape, he thought, with just a small bandage on his nose. *Where are we going? What kind of trip?*

They hadn't left the house since Ollie arrived, and he liked it here. And he liked her. But most nights, when he fell asleep, he thought about Nellie and John.

"We've got to go see Dr. Farley." She scooped him into her arms. "You might have an owner who is missing you."

I do, I do! Nellie and John. Was she taking him to see them?

He wagged his tail the whole time the lady dressed in her black cape and bonnet, then she slipped into her boots and retrieved her purse from the couch. There was a small red travel-sized kennel by the front door. It was almost exactly like the one Nellie and John used to put him in when they carted him around town. He didn't mind. When the buggies hit a rut, it could get bouncy, and he felt safe in the enclosure. *But wait . . .*

Ollie was pretty sure he'd been in a kennel like this when he'd lost track of Nellie and John. He remembered the man driving the car saying he wanted to get some coffee, so they'd stopped. Ollie had been given a snack and done his business. He'd fallen asleep after that.

The next thing he knew, there was fire, he was hurting, and he couldn't find Nellie and John.

He stopped wagging his tail, his recollections muddled now.

Once they got on the road, there was solace in the sound of the clip-clop of hooves, a familiar sound that lulled him into a tranquil state. But it wasn't long before they stopped in front of a small building. After Ollie was out of the kennel, the lady encircled his neck with a collar, then attached a leash and walked him inside. He'd never worn a collar. It felt foreign but not unpleasant.

She told the woman behind a glass window that she was here to see Dr. Farley, then she sat in one of the chairs in the room. Ollie tucked his tail between his legs from where he sat on the cold floor in front of her as he wondered which one of them needed doctoring.

He wasn't sure how much time had passed, but eventually a woman came from behind a door and waved her arm like she wanted them to follow her. So, they did.

They were led into a room like at the lady's house, but it was bigger. There was a metal table in the center, and there were shelves lined with equipment and bottles. Ollie tensed. He vaguely remembered being in a room like this when he was a puppy. And he was pretty sure there were shots involved. He didn't think he liked this place.

"Ada, Dr. Farley will be in shortly," the woman said, smiling before she left the room and closed the door behind her.

Ollie's ears perked up. *Ada.* Now he had a name for his new friend. *Ada, Ada, Ada*, he repeated over and over in his mind so he wouldn't forget.

But after that news sunk in, he began to shiver, a mixture of the cold temperature in the room and fear of being poked and prodded.

"You're okay, Ollie," Ada said.

Ada, Ada, Ada. He liked her name.

He wanted to believe her, that he was okay, that no harm would come to him—or to Ada.

A white-headed man entered the room, tall and stout, and without any warning whatsoever, he lifted Ollie into his arms and placed him on the cold metal table. He wasn't as gentle as Ada, but he did manage to avoid the tender spot on his belly. "Gloria said we're checking for a microchip today. I don't recognize this animal. If he has a chip, someone else must have inserted it."

"*Ya*." Ada cleared her throat. "He's a stray that I've had for a week. The weather wasn't *gut*, and he needed stitches. Today is the first day I felt like he was fit for travel."

Ollie wasn't sure if that was true. It seemed like the weather had been pretty good for a couple of days. At least better than it had been. Sunshine peeked through the clouds, lending a crisp breeze that made Ollie's fur fluffy.

"Can you please check him out thoroughly and make sure I didn't miss anything and that the place where I put stitches looks okay?"

Suddenly, Dr. Farley's hands were all over Ollie, and he offered up a low, guttural growl to let the older man know that he wasn't enjoying this. The doctor had to pry open Ollie's mouth to shine a light inside.

"Ada, you've done good work," the man said, still shining a light in Ollie's mouth. "I'm guessing he's around ten or eleven months old based on his size and his teeth."

Finally, Ollie was able to close his mouth. He eyed the distance from the table to the floor and decided that jumping down wasn't an option.

"I didn't think he was very old. He's playful and looks like he hasn't grown into his paws yet." Her voice sounded shaky as she spoke, then she dabbed at her eyes with a handkerchief she had in the pocket of her cape.

Dr. Farley had one hand on Ollie, as if to keep him from jumping down. Even though he'd decided against that, he wanted to be near Ada. Something was wrong with her. He could feel her sadness.

"Oh, dear. It looks like someone has gotten attached." The doctor began to stroke Ollie's back, and he wasn't sure if that motion was a trick or genuine. He remembered getting poked with a long needle once when a stranger stroked his back while he was atop a metal table.

"I guess I have gotten attached. But if he has owners who are missing him, then he should be returned." Ada swiped at her eyes with the tissue again.

Yes! Yes! I have owners. And I'm sure John and Nellie miss me!

"Well, let's have a look." The doctor took a step backward and picked up a round instrument, and Ollie held his breath and braced for whatever was coming, emitting a low growl since he was unsure. But the man only moved the round instrument all around Ollie's body—his neck, his back, and even down his legs.

Suddenly, there was a beep. Ada gasped before she covered her mouth with her hand, and her eyes got all wet.

"I need Gloria to run this registration number," Dr. Farley said. "I'll be back in a few minutes with the information."

After the door closed, Ada wrapped her arms around Ollie and took him off the table, putting him in her lap. She held him close and rubbed noses with him. A tear rolled down her cheek, and it made Ollie's heart hurt. He licked it away. *Why are you crying?*

"You'll be going home to your owners soon," she said.

Ollie's tail went into a full wag. *Nellie and John?* But then he looked up at Ada as another tear rolled down her

23

cheek. *Will I ever see her again?* That thought didn't make him feel very good.

"I wonder what your real name is," she said barely above a whisper.

It's Hank. But he wouldn't mind if she kept calling him Ollie if it would keep her from crying. He ran his tongue across her face, the same way he'd been doing every morning when he felt it was time for her to wake up. He'd been sleeping in her bed all week. But now, he just wanted to comfort her.

The gray-headed man—Dr. Farley—walked into the room a few moments later, his face ashen, his jowls drooping. He locked eyes with Ada. "This animal is registered to Nellie and John Troyer. It's odd that the name of the dog isn't included in the information, but he is registered to the Troyers."

Yes! Yes! They are my owners! Ollie wagged his tail. Soon, he'd be home. He glanced at Ada, who sniffled. Something tugged at his heart from deep inside.

Dr. Farley scratched his cheek as he shook his head. "I saw the article about the fatal accident in the local newspaper. Such a terrible thing to happen, especially so close to home." Sighing, he leaned against the counter and stuffed his hands in the pockets of his crisp white doctor's coat. "I remember reading that they didn't have any family who lived nearby."

Wait, wait, wait. What does 'fatal' mean?

Ada held Ollie a little closer. She smelled good, and he liked being with her, but he was confused about Nellie and John.

"I met Nellie and John's family while they were here

for the funeral." She glanced at Ollie. "Nellie and John had taken Ollie—or whatever his real name is—with them to Pennsylvania. He was in the car during their commute home when the car exploded in the ravine." She squeezed Ollie even closer. "He couldn't have survived." She blinked her eyes as she lifted her head to Dr. Farley's gaze. "This can't be the same dog."

Ollie listened, but he was having some strange flashbacks about what might have happened. *Screaming . . . the fire* . . . Had he flown in his kennel through the air?

The older man in the white coat said, "I had Gloria run the information twice on the scanner just to be sure. Maybe he was ejected out of the car before it . . . um, exploded."

Ada lowered her head, holding Ollie so tight he could barely breathe, but he didn't wiggle out of her embrace. She seemed to need him. "The right thing to do is to contact the extended family. Maybe they want him," Ada said, her voice still shaky.

"Do you have a way to reach them?" Dr. Farley leaned against the counter and folded his arms across his chest.

"*Ya*. They stayed at The Peony Inn. I'm sure Lizzie and Esther, the owners, have contact information."

"I know this is difficult, and I will pray for you, Ada."

After the doctor excused himself, citing other patients he needed to see, Ada put Ollie on the floor, secured his leash to his collar, and they left the building and headed toward her covered buggy.

She got him settled in the red carrier on the seat beside her, then she lowered her head into her hands and cried.

Ollie trembled all over. Ada was sad. And, if he'd heard and understood correctly, Nellie and John had crossed over their version of the rainbow bridge.

Are they gone forever?

Ollie's heart hurt in an unfamiliar way.

He glanced at Ada, who was still sobbing. He wanted out of the kennel. As much as he hurt, he wanted to comfort Ada. Apparently, she was in pain, too, and that tugged at his heart as much as the reality that he wouldn't see Nellie and John again.

Dogs don't cry the same way humans do, but Ollie was crying on the inside.

CHAPTER 5

*T*hey didn't go to Ada's home or to Ollie's. Instead, they went to a big house called The Peony Inn. Two nice older ladies named Esther and Lizzie ushered them into the living room. After the women consoled Ada, it was decided that they needed to make a phone call to a man named Jeremiah. The name was still familiar to Ollie, but he wasn't sure why.

Ada held Ollie in her lap, too tightly, but he allowed it as he tried to familiarize himself with this new place. He sniffed the air and liked the smells here. Cedar from the fireplace hung in the air with a background aroma of something yummy cooking in the oven.

The smaller of the two women punched buttons on the phone, then laid it down on the coffee table before she began to speak. "I know this might be hard to believe, but apparently John and Nellie's dog survived. I can't recall his name, but I know it's their dog because I saw him at their *haus*." The woman paused and drew in a deep breath before she went on. "It's a miracle, really."

That was the second time Ollie had heard the word 'miracle'.

The ladies huddled around the phone, and even though Ollie didn't understand exactly what was said, he'd gathered two things from the conversation. Nellie and John were not coming back for him. And a man named Jeremiah was coming to pick him up, presumably to take Ollie back to the place where he had vacationed with Nellie and John.

He recalled the house and the people they visited. They'd been nice. But there was a grouchy dog where they had vacationed. *Buster*. Ollie clenched his jaw as he recalled Buster's dislike of him, the way the big animal had bared his teeth and let it be known that Ollie was in his territory. *Is that where I'm going next?* He shivered at the possibility.

Ollie tuned out the rest of the conversation, mostly because he didn't understand it, and he'd gathered the information he needed as it pertained to him and his future. A future that didn't look bright.

As Ada continued to coddle him, Ollie decided that if he couldn't be with Nellie and John, he wanted to stay with her. Now, he wondered if that was even an option.

His insides began to settle after they'd left the big home and the two older women. A warm feeling washed over him when they arrived back at Ada's house after she'd offered him extra treats. Maybe she had sensed his anxiety. These weren't like regular treats from a box. Ada cooked treats for Ollie, and they tasted like peanut butter. He calmed down even more when they finally went to bed that evening. Ollie inched closer to her until she put her hand atop his head, then scratched behind his ears. "You're a *gut* boy, Ollie."

As good as her reassuring words and touch felt, his heart hurt for Nellie and John, and he worried about having to leave Ada to go away with the man named Jeremiah.

Ollie wasn't sleepy, and little by little, details were swimming into his mind filled with turbulence and heartbreak. *Nellie and John are gone.*

As Ada continued to stroke Ollie's back, he wondered if humans knew that dogs cried, even if only on the inside. And Ollie was sobbing buckets.

SEVERAL WEEKS PASSED before Jeremiah showed up at Ada's house one morning with a suitcase at his side. Ollie recognized him as one of the men they'd visited in Pennsylvania, donning a straw hat like their people wore. Now, he was here to pick up Ollie and take him to a faraway home that had only served as a vacation spot. A vacation spot that had housed a large dog that didn't care for Ollie at all. Ollie had tried to make friends, but the family pet, Buster, had no interest in forming a relationship. Just the opposite, Buster wanted Ollie gone.

Ada's house felt like home now, and Ollie had no plans to leave.

Ada held Ollie in her arms as she opened the front door. Even though Ollie recognized the man—Jeremiah— he didn't know him at all. He hadn't spent much time with him while he was in Pennsylvania with Nellie and John.

Jeremiah came and went as if he had another house somewhere. This man was a stranger.

"This is unbelievable." Jeremiah shook his head as he gazed at Ollie. "I don't know how to thank you for tending to Hank."

My name is Ollie now.

"Finding out that he was alive was the happiest I've seen *mei mamm* since Nellie and John died," Jeremiah said.

Ollie wondered who Jeremiah's mother was.

"I heard Lavina had liked this cute fellow." Ada leaned down and almost touched her nose to his snout, always careful of the small bandage that remained. Ollie loved it when she did that.

Lavina. He remembered her from their vacation. She was the mom of the family. A nice lady, but so was Ada, and Ollie didn't want to be relocated. He thought about Buster again and shivered.

"And you're welcome. I enjoyed taking care of him." She scratched Ollie behind his good ear as she continued to cradle him in one arm. "I have some medications I'd like to send with you. There are a few places that you still need to keep an eye on, and one spot on his nose that I've been trying to keep covered. Although he isn't fond of the bandage."

Because it itches.

Jeremiah followed her to the room with the metal table and the kennel. Ollie tensed when Ada gently set him on the cold table. "These are the spots I've been keeping a close eye on for infection, but so far, so *gut*." She took a deep breath and blew it out slowly. "And he loves to play fetch. I'll send the tennis ball that I bought for him with you."

No. I'm not going.

"*Ya*, great. I'll make sure he gets some play time and exercise while I'm here working on the *haus*. It needs some work before we can put it on the market for sale."

Here working on what house? Ollie assumed Jeremiah was taking him back to live with his family in Pennsylvania.

Ada began putting ointments and bandages in a bag.

Jeremiah picked up Ollie with no warning, his hand pressing across the sore spot on his belly. Ollie wanted to snap off his hand, but instead, he growled. Loudly.

"Uh oh," Jeremiah said.

And that was just a warning, Buddy.

Ada reached for Ollie, and his anxiety stilled in the comfort of her arms. "You can't hold him that way," she said rather loudly. "He is still tender right here." She maneuvered Ollie until the remnants of the healing wound on his underbelly were visible, still red with tufts of brown hair growing back and tiny holes where stitches had been. "I'm sorry if I sound snappy. I should have been more clear when I was explaining and showing you his injuries."

Or Jeremiah could have paid better attention. Ollie had seen the way Jeremiah looked at Ada the entire time she was trying to educate him. He'd been more interested in her as opposed to gathering a good understanding of Ollie's medical care.

Ada turned and left the room with Ollie against her chest and his paws propped up on her shoulder. Jeremiah followed. Ollie did his best to bare his teeth at the man as they walked. But it was a bit jarring when Ada thrust Ollie right into Jeremiah's arms when they got to the front door.

"Best of luck to you, and again . . . *mei* sympathies to you and your family." She gazed into Ollie's eyes. "Goodbye, Ollie . . . I mean, Hank."

But I'm Ollie now, remember?

Jeremiah eased backward over the threshold with a tight grip on Ollie. Ada closed the door.

What? Just like that? She's gone?

Ollie was too stunned to move as Jeremiah placed him on the ground, then attached a leash to his collar before picking up a piece of luggage he'd left on the porch, along with another small red suitcase that Ada had filled with medications and bandages. He began to lead Ollie away from Ada's house. Where was his buggy? Where was a car with a driver in it? *Are we going to walk? How far?* He looked over his shoulder. Ada was inside the house, staring out the window and touching her eyes with a tissue.

Don't let me go, Ada.

Ollie pulled against the leash and dug his heels into the snowy mush, wishing there was a way to fling some right into Jeremiah's face. But he barked instead, as loud as he could. And finally, Ada burst out the door and sprinted down the steps.

"Wait!" she yelled, and Ollie stopped barking and straining against the leash. "Didn't you arrange transportation?" she asked, breathless.

Ollie's hopes fell. He'd thought for sure Ada was

coming to take him back inside, that they'd cuddle up in her bed, and that he'd lick her face the next morning when it was time to get up. But he wasn't sure of anything anymore. He jerked the weight of his body until the leash broke free from Jeremiah's hand, then he ran to Ada. Losing Nellie and John had been awful. Ollie wasn't ready to lose Ada too.

"You silly boy," Ada said with her arms stretched wide to intercept him. She enclosed him in the safety of her arms, and he breathed in the smell of her, a mixture of lavender soap, cookies, and bread fresh from the oven. All aromas that Ollie loved, almost as much as he loved Ada. *Don't make me go.*

"Hank is attached to you," Jeremiah said. "I'm not surprised."

Ollie jerked his head around in time to see Jeremiah giving Ada that strange look again, almost like he was lovesick. John used to look at Nellie like that. But this man didn't even know Ada, did he? Ollie barked.

Ada stood up holding Ollie, and once again, for the time being, he felt safe. "He answers to Ollie now." She raised her chin and hugged Ollie closer.

Finally, she set him straight.

"Uh . . ." Jeremiah scratched his cheek, then tipped back the rim of his black hat. "Okay."

"I mean, I didn't know his name, so I just began calling him Ollie, and I think he's used to that." She sighed. "But he's your dog now, so I suppose you can call him whatever you'd like."

What is happening?

Ollie had heard Nellie say once that she was on an

33

emotional roller coaster. It had something to do with an argument with a friend. Ollie hadn't understood exactly what she meant until now. He wasn't sure what a roller coaster was, but he knew his emotions were all over the place.

Ollie twisted in Ada's arms to where he could keep an eye on Jeremiah, but Jeremiah only seemed to have eyes for Ada.

"I like the name Ollie." Jeremiah shrugged, smiling. "And I don't think it matters what we call hm. He clearly adores you."

Yes, so go home now. He turned and licked Ada on the cheek as a thank you.

She chuckled as she pressed her nose to Ollie's. "I've had him for a while." When she finished loving on Ollie, much too soon, she said, "You can't walk all the way to Nellie and John's *haus* balancing a dog on your hip or pulling him along on his leash while toting luggage."

Ollie's heart leapt. *Nellie and John's house?* Had he been wrong this entire time? Were Nellie and John at home waiting for his return? Soon, would he be back in his favorite chair?

"I-I can take you in *mei* buggy to Nellie and John's *haus* if you'd like."

Ollie's heart pounded against his chest. He didn't completely understand what was happening, but he was going home. And Ada was coming with him. He smiled on the inside, verging on happy tears as he swished his tail back and forth with absolute approval.

CHAPTER 6

*J*eremiah drove Ada's buggy, and Ollie got to ride in the front seat with Ada holding him. Ada had a bag of Ollie's favorite homemade treats, and she generously gave one to Ollie every time he looked up at her. He was fairly certain she could read his mind.

No one said much, and during the ride, Ada had slipped on a pair of dark sunglasses to cut the glare from the daytime sun, Ollie supposed. Or maybe she didn't want anyone to see her eyes. Nellie used to say that the eyes were the windows to the soul. Maybe she didn't want anyone to see her soul or how she was really feeling. She trembled ever so slightly. Jeremiah probably didn't notice, but Ollie did. He gave her a couple of big wet kisses which brought on a smile each time.

When they arrived at Nellie and John's house, a sense of familiarity filled Ollie with hope. But the yard was untended. John always cleared a neat path in the snow up to the porch, and there was never any of the white stuff on the porch. Today, there was no clear path, and a sludgy white and brown mess was half-melted on the porch.

No one got out of the buggy, and Ollie began to squirm, partly because he was anxious, but he also needed to do his business.

There was a long silence. Ollie wasn't sure what to think. But he wiggled in Ada's arms, hoping she'd get the message.

"Would you like for me to come in with you?" Ada finally asked.

Yes. Ollie was sure Nellie and John would be glad to see Ada too.

"I-I've already put you through enough." Jeremiah smiled, but it didn't look like a real smile to Ollie. He stepped out of the buggy and pulled his suitcases from the backseat. By the time he walked around to the other side of the buggy, Ada had already stepped out and set Ollie on the ground, grasping his leash as she shuffled to a dry patch of grass amid the driveway gravel, where Ollie was finally able to take care of business.

Afterward, Ada turned to Jeremiah and removed her sunglasses. Her eyes were red and moist. "I'll go in with you," she said with a tremor in her voice.

Even though his heart hurt for Ada, he couldn't wait to see John and Nellie, and he had a newfound bounce in his step as they crossed the yard and made their way up the porch steps.

Ada stepped to the side when they reached the front door. Jeremiah set down the suitcases, then fumbled in a side pocket of his jacket until he pulled out a key and unlocked the front door.

Ollie wagged his tail and panted with excitement. *I'm home*.

But it didn't feel like home as he crossed the threshold into the living room. He raised his snout and sniffed the air, then crinkled his nose. It didn't smell like home either. Nellie always had something baking in the oven, yummy aromas like at Ada's house. This house smelled stale, like the leftover smells from a fire.

Ada unhooked Ollie's leash from his collar before she said, "I'll start opening some windows to clear this stale air."

Jeremiah nodded as he took the grate from the fireplace and set it on the wood floor. Someone must have left the old wood and ashes, which caused the house to become stinky. That didn't sound like something Nellie or John would do.

Ollie stared at his chair, the one he slept in or sat on John's lap when he was home. He began to bark, assuming Nellie and John would have greeted him when he arrived. But as he ran from room to room downstairs, then jogged upstairs, it became clear that no one was home. In addition to the musty air, plumes of dust met with sunrays that shown through hazy windows in every room, dancing in circles around Ollie. He stood still in Nellie and John's bedroom. There weren't any sheets on the bed, and where was the pretty pastel quilt that covered the bed? Ollie eyed the far-left corner at the foot of the bed where he used to sleep.

There was no life in this room. As he rechecked the other upstairs rooms, then the downstairs, the realization hit that his first thoughts had been correct. Nellie and John had left him for good.

Ollie still had one place to check. He ran to the kitchen, but instead of Nellie or John, he found Ada moving things around and tossing items in the trashcan. Ollie walked to his food and water bowls, both with his name from his past life etched into the plastic. A life not so long ago that seemed to collide with whatever was going on now. He stared at the name on both bowls. *Hank*. But Hank wasn't Hank without Nellie and John.

He glanced up at Ada and wished she could read his mind.

"I know you must be hungry," she said as she reached down and scratched him behind the ears. "And you're being so patient, but I haven't found any dog food yet."

Ollie wasn't hungry. He was confused and scared. Would he be left in this house that now felt like a shell of his former home—a house that smelled bad and with a man he didn't know?

He followed Ada to the living room. Jeremiah had started a new fire, and it smelled more normal to Ollie, but sadness overtook him, and he retreated to the recliner, which used to be his favorite spot in the house. He wasn't sure anymore.

Ollie listened to Ada and Jeremiah talking, and he picked up as much as he could. Nellie and John had died, and Ada would be leaving soon. Ollie would be left here with Jeremiah with nothing familiar but the house and furniture, which didn't compare to the warmth of human companionship from those he knew and trusted.

When Ada picked up her purse, Ollie began to weep on the inside again. *Please don't leave me.*

She was almost to the door when she looked over her shoulder twice at Ollie, locking eyes with him the second time. Her bottom lip trembled, and Ollie didn't want to look away from her, but when he did, he saw that Jeremiah was staring at her while rubbing his chin. Was it hard for Ada to leave Ollie too? Was Jeremiah picking up on that?

The stranger in Ollie's house yawned. "I'm exhausted. I believe the *Englisch* call it jet lag. And since we didn't find any food for Ollie, maybe you could keep him tonight?" He raised an eyebrow.

Ollie straightened as his ears perked up. *Say yes.* As much as he loved this house, it wasn't a home without Nellie and John. And he knew Ada cared about him.

He held his breath and waited. When Ada called his name and squatted down, he ran into her arms, the safest place he knew in the world these days.

Ada and Jeremiah talked, something about going to the store the following day, which caused his stomach to clench until he heard that he would be able to go with them. Right now, he didn't want to be far from Ada, and he was unsure what he would do if anything happened to her as well.

When they got back to Ada's house, they both ate. She doctored Ollie's nose, and after she had showered, they crawled into bed just like they'd been doing for over a month. Ollie didn't want to go back to Nellie and John's house without them there. This was his new home now, and with that thought, he fell asleep quickly, but he still thought about Nellie and John before he dozed off.

The next morning, Ada put Ollie in the portable red kennel in the backseat of her covered buggy. He would rather be on her lap, but he recalled the conversation between Ada and Jeremiah the day before. They were going to pick up Jeremiah and go to the store.

Jeremiah was waiting on the front porch of what used to be Ollie's home when Ada pulled in. He climbed into the passenger side, meaning there was no chance Ollie could ride in Ada's lap. But, from his kennel, he could see out the side window of the buggy. They passed farms and other buggies, and a few cars blew past them. Cars had always scared Ollie. Even more so now. They were big and fast. He cringed every time when they passed in the other lane, and he closed his eyes when a car sped from behind the buggy and went around them.

Ada and Jeremiah talked a lot. Ada even laughed a few times. It seemed like they were becoming friends. Or maybe more than friends. Ollie wasn't sure how he felt about that yet.

Finally, they arrived at the store, and while Ada bundled her cape more tightly around her waist, Jeremiah tethered the horse, then reached into the kennel and picked up Ollie. He yelped. The man didn't know how to hold him without hitting the sore spot on his belly, and he wanted Ada to carry him.

"Uh, oh." Jeremiah frowned. "Did I do something to hurt him or pick him up wrong again? Maybe he's not completely healed?"

Ollie seethed on the inside, stifling a grumble. He'd been shown how to hold Ollie before. Didn't he listen?

"He might still be sore, but he should be fine." Ada reached out her arms, and Ollie wasted no time wiggling out of Jeremiah's hold on him.

"He's attached to you," Jeremiah said again.

Yes. Ollie snuggled into Ada's arms.

"Maybe," she said. "I've had him for a while. And, surprisingly, no one has brought any other animals for me to tend to, so *mei* attention has been solely on him."

As it should be. He licked her on the face, and she smiled.

Ollie had only been around one other dog, and it had been while he was vacationing with Nellie and John—that big dog, Buster, who liked to show off his sharp teeth.

Inside the store, Jeremiah and Ada were talking to two ladies dressed the same way as Ada. Ollie took the opportunity to look around from his perch inside a metal shopping cart. There were all kinds of things to see. Food, clothes, and even toys. He wagged his tail.

Then he saw it . . .

Another dog in the store. The small canine was in the arms of a woman with a lot of wrinkles on her face, and when Ollie looked his way, he puckered up his little face and snarled. It reminded Ollie of the mean dog in Pennsylvania even though he was small.

Ollie leapt from the shopping cart he'd been riding in, forgetting he was still sore. After a yelp from the pain, he ran to the woman, jumped up, and nipped at her dress. He didn't want to hurt her, but he thought he might nip at the tiny dog in her arms for giving him such a vicious look.

"Ollie! *Nee!*" Ada rushed to the woman, but Jeremiah darted past her and scooped Ollie into his arms. Then it all happened so fast!

Ollie didn't mean to bite Jeremiah, but he picked him up the wrong way again. *Won't he ever learn?* Ada was talking with the woman and her vicious little dog. Jeremiah was bleeding.

And worst of all . . . Ada scowled at Ollie, which caused his heart to hurt.

I'm sorry I was bad.

CHAPTER 7

*L*ater, they were back at Nellie and John's house, following a quiet ride, Ada cleaned and bandaged Jeremiah's wound where Ollie had bitten him. Ollie wished they knew how sorry he was. Maybe that's why he wasn't getting very much attention from anyone. He'd curled up in what used to be his favorite recliner, but this was a confusing time for him. *Is this home, or is Ada's house supposed to be my home?*

Either way, Ada was on the couch with Jeremiah, and they kept talking and talking and even moved closer to each other—almost like Ollie wasn't even there. Jeremiah smiled a lot. Ada batted her eyes at him.

What's happening?

Ollie jumped from the chair, then trotted his way across the living room, eyeing Jeremiah along the way. He raised his chin, did his best to squint his eyes at the man, then he eased into Ada's lap. He was mindful of his tummy, which was sorer after he had bolted from the shopping cart earlier.

Jeremiah scratched him behind his ears, and he had to admit that felt good. "He is a cutie," he said, causing Ollie to rethink his opinion about Jeremiah. He'd heard Nellie say that jealousy is a sin.

He did feel badly for biting Jeremiah and that he'd upset Ada. Maybe he could learn to like Jeremiah as much as he did Ada. That's how it had happened with Nellie and John. He'd adored Nellie from the beginning, but it took Ollie a while to warm up to John.

Nellie and John. Gone.

He nuzzled closer to Ada and tried to push their memory aside. He dozed off in his new owner's lap, but he awoke suddenly when she stood and carried him into the kitchen. Ollie could hear Jeremiah on the phone in the other room. Ada carefully set him on the floor in front of his food and water bowls.

But I'm not hungry or thirsty.

He gazed up at her, wondering why she'd abruptly stood and carried him to the kitchen. When she squatted down, a tear ran down her cheek while her lip trembled. Instinctively, Ollie licked her tear away. Was she crying because Ollie had misbehaved today in the store? He thought they were past that.

Jeremiah walked into the kitchen, then when Ada stood, he hugged her. Ollie wasn't sure how to feel. Part of him wanted to step in between Jeremiah and Ada but he decided against it since when Jeremiah hugged Ada, Ollie sensed that it made her feel better. She melted into his embrace.

"I shouldn't have gotten so attached to Ollie because I

knew he might belong to someone else or that Nellie and John's next of kin might want him. But I know having him checked for a chip was the right thing to do." Ada leaned into Jeremiah's arms.

Someone else? What?

Then Ada and Jeremiah began to kiss and hug a lot, for a while. It reminded Ollie of Nellie and John when they were a family. Maybe this was Ollie's new family, both Ada and Jeremiah.

But where will we all live? Here? At Ada's house? And why did she mention me belonging to someone else?

Ollie was caring less and less about where they lived if he was with Ada. And Ada seemed to enjoy having Jeremiah around, so Ollie would learn to love him, too, just like he'd done with John.

OVER THE NEXT couple of weeks, Ollie, Ada, and Jeremiah had settled into a routine. Ollie didn't completely understand it, but he liked it. He and Ada spent their days with Jeremiah. Sometimes they went shopping. Ollie tried to ignore other dogs so as not to upset anyone. It seemed best that way even though the hair on his back rose if another canine sniffed the air or perked his ears. Ada and Jeremiah also cleaned the property where Jeremiah was staying. The whole space took on a freshness and new life, and although it was starting to feel like Jeremiah and Ada's house, there was still one exception.

Every night before it got dark, Ada would give Jeremiah a long, affectionate hug before taking Ollie back to her house, where just Ollie and Ada would sleep. It was like having two homes, and that was okay with Ollie. Until one day everything changed, veered from the pattern he had become used to . . . and enjoyed.

Ada took Ollie off her lap and took him to his recliner, then swiped at her eyes. "It's going to be dark soon," she said to Jeremiah over her shoulder, sniffling.

Ollie wasn't sure why Ada was unhappy, but he was ready to go to his other home if something was upsetting her here.

Ada leaned down, kissed Ollie on his forehead, and through tears, she said, "I will miss you, Ollie, but you will have a new home with people who will *lieb* you the way I have . . . and the way Nellie and John did."

What? What? What? Ollie didn't always understand everything his humans said, but he perceived this conversation to be some sort of goodbye, which caused his chest to tighten as he began to pant, an effort to calm himself, which wasn't working.

After Ada stood, Jeremiah held her cheeks between his hands and kissed her. Ollie was getting used to this affectionate behavior, but he wasn't used to seeing Ada cry any more.

"I have to go." Ada eased out of Jeremiah's embrace and glanced out the window. "It will be dark soon," she said again.

Right, dark. We must go to our other home.

Ollie jumped from the recliner, stood wagging his tail, and waited to follow Ada to the door after she stopped hugging and kissing Jeremiah.

But following another long kiss at the door, Ada rushed outside, closing the door behind her and leaving Ollie alone with Jeremiah. Ollie's heart flipped in his chest, and not in a good way. He jumped up on the couch and propped his front paws on the back of the cushion to get a better view out the window, unable to stop himself from whimpering. *Ada, come back! Don't leave me!* He whimpered louder.

"I know, fella. *Mei* heart is breaking too." Jeremiah lifted Ollie into his arms, not the correct way, but better. Ollie wanted to know why he wasn't going with Ada like he did every night. "But *mei mamm*, Lavina, is really looking forward to you living with her," Jeremiah said. "It will be like a part of Nellie and John are still with her." Jeremiah paused, sighing. "And we've finished all the work and cleaning on the *haus* so we can sell it."

Ollie liked when humans addressed him as if he were one of them, but this news left an uncertain outcome.

Jeremiah carried Ollie to his bed and patted the extra pillow. "Get comfy while I take a shower."

Get comfy? Where is Ada?

Ollie waited until Jeremiah was out of sight before he leapt from the bed and trotted back to the living room. He resumed his position on the couch, his front paws pressing against the back cushion as he looked out into a star-filled night, unable to stop whimpering. Ada was gone.

He heard Jeremiah talking to someone on the phone a while later and didn't understand what was happening. But when Jeremiah said, "*Gut nacht, Mamm.* Ollie and I will see you tomorrow evening," Ollie held his breath and waited for more.

But Jeremiah placed the phone on the coffee table, then he picked up Ollie and carried him back to the bedroom. Ollie wanted to run back to the couch to keep watching for Ada to return, but when Jeremiah swiped at his eyes, Ollie's heart warmed toward the man.

He wasn't sure what was happening, but it seemed to Ollie that Jeremiah might be almost as sad as Ollie was, so he decided to sleep in his bed . . . just this one night . . . until he could get home to Ada.

THE NEXT MORNING, Ollie wasn't hungry and stood staring at his bowls filled with food and water.

"What's the matter, fella?" Jeremiah asked from where he was sitting at the kitchen table eating breakfast. "Aren't you hungry?"

No. I'm not. I'm confused and unhappy. Where's Ada?

Jeremiah stood, still chewing, and took two pieces of bacon, crumbled it up, and added it to Ollie's food bowl.

Sad as he was, bacon was an addiction, and he devoured all his food.

The next thing he knew, he was in one of Ada's portable kennels and in the backseat of a car driven by a man he didn't know. Jeremiah sat up front with the stranger, making Ollie feel even worse than he already did. As much as he wanted to stay awake, his eyes were as heavy as his heart. Where was Jeremiah taking him?

Ollie dozed on and off, feeling full as a tick from eating too much. But during his waking moments, his eyes searched for Ada—within the car and outside as they drove. The landscape was becoming unfamiliar, not like where Ada and Jeremiah lived. They left behind fields with farmhouses and buggies traveling on the roads to a busy highway with lots of cars and big trucks. Where was Jeremiah taking him? When would they return? His heart ached, but he kept unwillingly drifting back to sleep. A full belly had that effect.

He had no idea how long they had been in the van when they finally came to a stop and the driver turned off the engine. Nightfall had set in, and Ollie strained his neck from his spot in the kennel. He could see outside where big lamps lit the yard around him.

Where am I?

Jeremiah unloaded his suitcases and some boxes and set them on the ground.

What about me? Ollie's breathing became ragged, and he was starting to panic. He didn't know the man driving the car. Was Jeremiah going to leave him too? Ollie felt tears welling in the corners of his eyes, the ones humans didn't see, and he began to tremble.

Then familiar strong hands unhooked the latch on the kennel, and Jeremiah carefully lifted him out, the correct way this time. Ollie couldn't stop panting, but he did give Jeremiah a quick lick on the face, so he'd know he was grateful not to be forgotten and left in the vehicle. All this change was too much to handle.

Jeremiah thanked the man for transporting them, as the man helped by carrying the luggage and boxes to the front porch. Jeremiah followed toward the house with Ollie still in his arms.

They were on their way up the porch steps when Ollie realized where he was.

Oh no.

CHAPTER 8

*U*pon arrival, Ollie recognized where he was, and this was Buster's territory. The Blue Heeler made it clear to Ollie that he was an intruder in his home, though Ollie tried to assure him that he had no say in the matter. Ollie simply wanted to get along, and even offered to share his ball with Buster. One morning, Ollie reluctantly, offered up some bacon Lavina had given him with breakfast. Buster snatched the bacon from Ollie's bowl, but it didn't change things between them. Buster was the boss in this household, and he continued to snarl, growl, and bare his teeth to let him know he was the alpha. Ollie tried to find solace in the woman named Lavina, who was nice to Ollie over the next few weeks. He remembered being in this house with Nellie and John on vacation before his life was turned upside down.

Jeremiah didn't live in the house, and he only stopped by occasionally, giving him a familiar scratch behind the ears, though he often came bearing treats. Perhaps Jeremiah had forgotten about Ada, but Ollie couldn't shrug off the memory of the woman who saved his life. He missed sleeping on her bed, how she smelled like lavender, and the aroma of something freshly baked lingering in the air. Sometimes, it smelled like his peanut butter treats. That was his home. Second to that had been Nellie and John's house where Jeremiah, Ada, and Ollie had spent so much time together.

Where he lived now did not feel like home. Ollie spent most of his time avoiding Buster.

Ollie had brief moments of joy when Lavina cuddled him in her lap, but mostly he stayed on edge, worried if Buster was lurking nearby. Even though the other canine was constantly being reprimanded for his behavior toward Ollie, things were not getting any better. He missed Ada, and he didn't understand how she could just let him leave. Ollie had seen the sadness in her eyes, witnessed her tears. He would never understand humans. Didn't she realize that Ollie would have done anything for her? Didn't she know how much he loved her?

Today, Buster was out in the barn with Elijah Huyard, the man of the house, while Ollie snuggled up on a blanket on the couch. He tried to sleep. It was the only time he didn't think about his past lives. He'd heard that cats had nine lives, so maybe dogs did too. But Ollie wasn't enjoying this particular life.

Jeremiah walked into the room, and Ollie's ears perked up. Over the weeks since he'd been here, Jeremiah had continued to bring him treats whenever he stopped by to visit his parents, Lavina and Elijah, and he always took time to pet Ollie. They weren't as tasty as the treats Ada had made for him, but Ollie appreciated the gestures.

Ollie had been fortunate to have so many people love him, but he still held a fondness for Nellie and John, even though he knew from Lavina's whispered prayers late at night that they weren't coming back into his life. They were with God. But surely God wouldn't have taken away Ada too. Ollie wished Jeremiah would just take him back to Ada's house so he could give her some comfort as well.

As Jeremiah and his mother chatted, Ollie yawned.

"*Mamm*, even if that were the case, I have a *haus* and a job here. Ada has a *haus* and a great community where she lives," Jeremiah said to his mother. Ollie was suddenly wide awake when he heard Ada's name as he raised an ear to hear better. "It's just not geographically possible for us to share a life together."

Yes, it is! Ollie nodded, but no one seemed to notice.

"*Gott* has a way of turning tragedy into *gut*," Lavina said. "If sweet Ollie hadn't survived, you probably wouldn't have spent so much time with Ada. And the way you've been moping around since you returned home tells me that you miss her."

Ollie rarely heard them talk about Ada, and even though he didn't always understand the conversations going on around him, he tried to fine tune what they were saying. Lavina's eyes were moist. Ollie was tempted to nuzzle her, to smother her with kisses, and let her know he was here for her even if he didn't want to be. But he didn't want to interrupt their conversation since they were talking about his beloved Ada.

"All things are possible when you draw on the strength of Christ. And when *Gott* opens a door, it's always a path that *He* has chosen for you." Lavina swiped at her eyes.

"*Sohn* . . . life is short." Lavina paused, sniffling. "I don't want you to waste a minute of yours."

Jeremiah sighed. "*Mamm*, I *lieb* you, and I can see where you are going with this, but it's an impossible situation."

Lavina blinked her eyes a few times, but then she smiled. "Nothing is impossible."

Jeremiah shook his head and left the room. Lavina stood for a moment with her head slumped before she also exited the den. And Ollie was left alone with his thoughts, unsure of his future, but keeping one eye open, the way he always did, in case Buster found his way into the room.

It was a few weeks later when Jeremiah packed Ollie into the kennel that he'd brought him in to Lavina's house and loaded Ollie into a van like the one he'd arrived in. Jeremiah had also packed a lot of boxes in the vehicle as if this wasn't going to be a quick trip to the market or to visit friends.

Lavina had coddled him, kissed him on his snout, and tearfully told him she would miss him. While there was a sense of relief that he might finally be away from Buster, he liked Lavina. "You've brought me so much comfort, Ollie. A connection to Nellie and John. But someone else needs you more than I do."

Who? What does that mean? Where are you taking me now? How many homes will I have before I'm part of a real family? Ollie felt like the baggage piled all around, just something else to be hauled off. He covered his face with his paws inside the kennel as the man driving started the motor on the car. Ollie felt spent, the same way he was when he'd left Ada behind. He could only assume that this would be another long ride.

The driver stopped twice en route to wherever they were headed so that Jeremiah could let Ollie out to do his business, but he felt sluggish. At least there was a soft, warm blanket inside the kennel that he could use to help him sleep during this long ride.

When they finally arrived at their destination, Ollie felt alert for the first time because he couldn't believe what he was seeing. They were back at Nellie and John's house. He'd given up hope that he would ever see his first family, but would Ada be inside? His heart leapt at the thought.

After Jeremiah took him from the kennel and set him on the ground, Ollie took off across the yard and trotted up the porch steps, wagging his tail, barking with all the energy he possessed.

"You recognize this place, Ollie?" Jeremiah asked as he balanced a box on one hip while he unlocked the door.

Ollie brushed past Jeremiah, crossed over the threshold, then ran from room to room downstairs before giving the upstairs equal attention. He wanted to shout Ada's name, but instead he barked so she would know he was home.

After a complete inspection, he jumped up on the familiar recliner, covered his snout with his paws, and cried on the inside. *Ada isn't here.* And, as happy as he was to be back in his original house, it didn't feel like a home without Ada. Ollie decided he should be grateful to Jeremiah for bringing him back here, but was this only a temporary trip? Would he be ripped away from the familiarity he craved?

Later in the afternoon, a big truck pulled into the driveway. It was so large that it barely fit in the space. When men started moving furniture into the house, Ollie's hope skyrocketed. This appeared to be a permanent move. Surely Ada would be here soon too.

When Jeremiah spooned food into one bowl and filled the second one with water, Ollie finally had an appetite and scarfed down what he'd been offered, lapping up water when he was done. He cringed at the name Hank still on his bowls, but he could live with that if Ada would just come home.

It was a busy day with furniture being moved out and other household items being moved in. Ollie stayed in his recliner, fearful the people moving furniture would try to take his chair. He spread out his paws against the cushion to claim it every time someone came close. He was prepared to defend his spot, although his growling days were behind him. He'd leave that business to Buster.

Hours went by and no Ada. Jeremiah fed Ollie again, although he wasn't as hungry this evening. He cared for Jeremiah, and he was happy to be back in Nellie and John's house, but his person was missing.

"I bet you're happy to be back here and away from Buster," Jeremiah said to Ollie as he carried him to the bedroom and placed him on the bed.

Yes, I am. But Ollie had only spent a few nights at the foot of this bed, and then, he'd been taken far away to a house where he'd never fully belonged—with a Blue Heeler who didn't want him as a playmate. Would he be whisked away tomorrow morning? Again? He wasn't sure he would survive another move, especially if he was being shipped to strangers. Why didn't anyone permanently want him?

Ollie had watched his humans press their palms together, then talk to someone called God, who seemed to be very important. They didn't always talk out loud, but when they did, they thanked God for things like the food on the table and special things that happened that day. They also asked Him for things, such as blessings for their harvest, good health for their family, and they always promised that they would try to live their lives based on goodness and God's will.

As nightfall came, Ollie had lost hope that Ada would be joining them. She'd had plenty of time to visit Ollie, and it was a short drive by buggy to her house. Ollie's heart sunk even more with the realization that Ada must not love him as much as he loved her.

After Jeremiah began to snore, unaware that Ollie was crying on the inside, he decided to try something new. He closed his eyes and spoke to God in his mind, the way he'd heard others speak aloud.

Dear Gott, *thank you for bringing me back to Nellie and John's house. Please don't let Jeremiah send me away tomorrow. I will live here without Ada if that is Your will. But can I ask You to please bring her back to me?*

He didn't know if his request would be honored, but a warm feeling came over him, a suggestion of sorts that everything might be all right.

Ollie awoke the next morning to the sound of voices, but he wasn't motivated to jump off the bed. He'd tossed and turned all night, worrying and curious about this new housing situation, despite that warm feeling that had settled over him. But his chest tightened when he finally yawned and realized the bedroom door was closed. Where was Jeremiah? Why was Ollie confined to the bedroom? Panic rose up through his chest, and his temptation to bark was overwhelming, but instead he hopped from the bed and tiptoed on his paws to the door to listen to the voices.

He recognized Jeremiah talking. "I *lieb* you, Ada. I've *liebed* you from the first moment I saw you." Ollie's tail wagged so hard that he thought it might snap in two, but he needed to hear the rest before he let himself get too excited. Then their voices got muffled. *What's happening?*

He barked as loud as he could so Ada would hear him. Moments later, the door flung open, and Jeremiah was smiling broadly. "She's here, Ollie."

He ran with all his might, slipping and sliding on the wood floors, but when he saw Ada kneeling down with her arms wide open, Ollie thought his heart might explode as he jumped into her arms. His Ada began to cry. "*Ach, mei* sweet boy. I've missed you!" Ollie covered her in wet kisses. *I've missed you too!*

After Ada had officially welcomed him back, she lifted him into her arms and turned to Jeremiah. "But what about your *mamm*? I thought Ollie brought her comfort?"

"*Mamm liebed* Ollie, but *mei daed's* dog, Buster, wasn't having any part of Ollie," Jeremiah said.

No kidding! Ollie showered Ada with more kisses.

"And *Mamm* knew how hard it was for you to say goodbye to Ollie, so she wanted you to have him." Jeremiah smiled as he reached over and scratched Ollie behind his ears. "*Mamm* knew that me living in Nellie and John's *haus* was like having a part of them still with us. But that wasn't *mei* main reason for buying this *haus*, and I think you know that." He leaned around Ollie and kissed Ada for a long time. Ollie didn't think he would have shared Ada with anyone other than Jeremiah. He had missed her too.

I'm home.

EPILOGUE

For six months, things went back to normal. Ollie stayed with Ada during the evenings, and when Jeremiah wasn't working, they spent time with him during the day.

Ollie had learned to fetch his tennis balls even better. He had four of them now. His food and water bowls now said Ollie instead of Hank. And there was always an abundance of Ada's peanut butter treats. Sometimes, he even got bacon with his breakfast.

Ada worked sometimes too. She took care of other animals. At first Ollie wasn't happy that other animals were in the house, but he didn't want to act like Buster. Instead, he learned to adjust when he began to understand that Ada helped these other furry critters the same way that she had helped him. But when they were well, they went back to their own homes with their owners. A few really sick animals stayed overnight, but mostly Ollie stayed by Ada's side.

Then, one day, the most wonderful thing happened.

Jeremiah and Ada got married, and they all three lived at Jeremiah's house. They renovated Ada's smaller house into a veterinarian's office and shelter for homeless animals. Ada still cared for animals when she could, but she hired someone with an animal science degree as an assistant technician, so she'd have more time to be a wife.

Ollie had settled into a life of options. Sometimes, he went to work with Ada when she chose to go. Other days, he stayed with Jeremiah out in the workshop.

He'd heard Ada, Jeremiah, and others say that God created miracles out of tragedy. Ollie was older and understood a little more about that now. He still thought about Nellie and John, but there was comfort living in their home.

Ollie recalled his prayer to God, knowing He must have heard Him because He answered by giving Ollie his forever home. Ollie had heard Ada tell Jeremiah that while they could never understand the things God does in our lives, He is always working for our good. Ollie agreed and prayed that he would always be with Ada and Jeremiah, that he would never take their love for granted.

OLLIE'S PEANUT BUTTER TREATS

<u>Ingredients</u>
- 1 cup toasted wheat germ
- 2 cups flour (whole wheat)
- 1/2 tsp. ground cinnamon
- 3/4 cup water
- 1/4 cup peanut butter (creamy)
- 1 large egg
- 2 T. Canola oil

<u>Instructions</u>

Preheat thevoven to 350 degrees. Combine wheat germ, flour, and cinnamon, then stir in remaining ingredients. Roll dough out on a floured surface to 1/4" thickness. Cut cookies using a 3" bone-shaped cookie cutter.

Place cookies two inches apart on an ungreased baking sheet. Bake 30-35 minutes until bottoms are lightly browned. Cool thoroughly on a wire rack.

A REQUEST

Authors depend on reviews from readers. If you enjoyed this book, would you please consider leaving a review on Amazon?

FREE DOWNLOAD

If you would like to subscribe to my newsletter and receive a FREE short story, go to www.bethwiseman.com. I only send ONE newsletter per month.

AND TURN THE PAGE IF YOU WOULD LIKE TO READ A SAMPLE OF THE BESTSELLER—*THE MESSENGER.*

THE MESSENGER

BETH WISEMAN

BESTSELLING & AWARD-WINNING AUTHOR

THE MESSENGER - PROLOGUE

Dying is a beautiful thing, especially at my age when the body no longer functions the way it should. I suffered through decades of arthritis that made me want to take a jackhammer to my knees. Then, a heart attack, two bypasses, esophageal cancer, and a life-threatening case of pneumonia almost took me down, but in the end, it was a bee sting. Yep, that's right—a wicked case of anaphylactic shock, which left me gasping for air on my living room floor until my granddaughter found me and rushed me to the emergency room. I was more than ready to go at age eighty-two when I heard that monitor flatline, knowing I'd soon see my beloved Mary Grace and my daughter, Lydia, who had passed away much too young. Cancer plagued our family, and I always assumed that's how I would go. Or maybe heart failure. My ticker wasn't what it should be, either. A bee sting wouldn't have been in my top one hundred causes of death.

Leaving my earthly existence happened as I had imagined, although the white light was a mixture of brilliant hues that I believe must have included every color in the rainbow, heavy on golden shades of yellow. I saw Mary Grace as my soul left my worn-out body on the hospital bed. She looked the same as the day I married her—tight blonde curls, a dimply smile, and sapphire eyes that lit up a room. Her presence immediately left me wondering what I looked like. Was I now the handsome young lad she'd married fifty-eight years ago? Or had I ascended into the next life as my slumped-over gray-haired self who walked with a limp?

Lydia was a beautiful woman in her twenties, cancer-free and glowing with good health. I was filled with a love I'd never felt as I glided along the well-lit path. It was like levitating barely off the ground toward a destiny that would forever fill me with contentment and peace.

If there was a downside to exiting my earthly existence, it was my granddaughter—Amelia—whom I was leaving behind. A woman in her early forties raising a troubled son. Amelia was good to me right up until the end, and I worried for her and Michael, her only child. The boy had been in and out of juvenile detention centers and had already caused his mother a lifetime of heartache by the age of seventeen.

But even my anxiety about leaving them wasn't enough to pull me from the euphoric state of mind that lured me toward my departed loved ones. I had waited for this moment to lay eyes on my family, to glide toward them without having any pain. Mary Grace was the first to greet me, wrapping her arms around me, no words necessary, as I could feel her every emotion radiate through my being. I was home.

Lydia was the next person to welcome me, and again, no words were needed. In the distance, I saw my parents, my brother Edwin, coworkers I remembered warmly, friends and neighbors who had come home before me, and other folks I hadn't seen in decades but of whom I had fond recollections. They'd all been waiting for me, and it was a reunion like no other. Again, it was everything I had imagined, short of one thing. I was hungry. Famished. I searched for a glorious spread of food that might be laid out by my welcoming party, but all I saw in front of me was the rainbow of lights and my family and friends.

My stomach growled, which seemed odd. I was in Heaven, but apparently there was food in Heaven, or I wouldn't be feeling this mild annoyance. I wondered if I would eventually be offered a juicy red steak complemented by a fully loaded baked potato. Perhaps even a slice of red velvet cake loaded with cream cheese icing and a side of vanilla ice cream. My favorites, but the food I'd steered away from since Amelia had insisted that I partake in a heart-healthy diet.

Flanked by family and friends, I kept floating toward the golden gates, and as I neared, they opened with ease, and a new sort of light met me on the other side. I knew immediately what—and who—the light was, and I dropped to my knees and lowered my head, unworthy to face the Son of God or even be in His presence. I wept with feelings of gratitude and remorse over things I'd done in my life, but I mostly absorbed His love like a sponge that had been dry until this moment in time.

My family and friends dispersed before I was ready for them to go, but I suppose this was the point when I faced all my wrongdoings head-on, begged to be absolved of my sins, and embraced my Lord and Savior with all the love in my heart. But my stomach wouldn't stop growling, which was a distraction at the very least.

When a hand cupped my chin and eased me to my feet, I stood and gazed upon Jesus. I instinctively embraced Him. Every sin I'd ever committed slapped me in the face like a wet rag, unpleasant but not hurtful. I wanted to stay in His arms forever, but when my stomach grumbled even louder, I knew something was amiss. Jesus asked me to walk with Him, although it wasn't really walking. It was like skating without skates, not gliding or floating. It was different than earlier.

Jesus communicated to me without speaking, and I knew that ahead of me was God. Nothing in my life could have prepared me for this moment, and the peaceful calm I'd always envisioned wrapped around me like a blanket of bliss, perfect in every way. Except for my hunger pains, which continued to confuse me.

As I took a seat next to my Heavenly Father, I couldn't remember the last time I'd sat without my knees throbbing with pain. I was especially grateful for the Lord's mercy and my pain-free new existence.

God began to communicate with me using words. His voice was deep, which might have sounded threatening if He hadn't been who He was. Or perhaps I had been wrong in my assumptions. Maybe I should have felt threatened. I hadn't done anything awful, like kill anyone or intentionally cause harm to another person, but I'd committed my fair share of sins. Despite the love I felt, I braced myself for what was to come. All the while, visions of steak and baked potatoes filled my senses with guilt, knowing I shouldn't be thinking of such things right now.

"Walter, I've been waiting for you," God said in His deep voice. "You're very special to me."

I swallowed hard, surprised that, despite my painless existence, I had a lump in my throat. It was accompanied by the guilt I felt as I wondered if He said that to everyone. Or was I really special? God smiled. I think.

"But you can't stay." God spoke firmly, and tears welled at the corners of my eyes. Had I miscalculated my misdeeds? Was I going to the other place instead?

"Why?" My voice sounded like that of a child pleading with his mother about why he couldn't go to the playground or something equally as unmatched as this conversation.

"There are things I need you to do before you take permanent residence here." God spoke firmly, but I'd never been so relieved in my life. At least I would be returning. But I stiffened and said the first thing that came to mind.

"I don't want to go back. I want to stay here." Was this going to be a debate? Was I expected to plead my case? I felt sure I would lose for all the obvious reasons.

"I know you don't want to leave, but it is necessary." God placed a soothing hand on my shoulder. "You will return to your earthly home with renewed health, and you will hear My voice in your mind, directing you to do My will."

"Huh?" I tried to swallow that lump in my throat again as I blinked back tears. *Why me?*

"There are those who cannot—or choose not to—hear My voice. They have blocked My guidance in their lives out of fear, worry, anxiety, or disbelief. But I love all My children, and I want to save as many as I can."

I wanted to ask God how I factored into what He was saying, but I knew right away that He knew what I was thinking.

"When you return in the grandest of health, you will meet people who need to hear what I have to say in order to find their way to Me. I will guide you in this endeavor. Just listen for My voice the way you always have."

How many times had I felt the Lord guiding me? Is that what He meant?

"Yes," He said right away. "You will find yourself in situations, often with strangers, that will require you to spread My messages in an effort to help that person shed the suffering he or she is feeling, to forgo their fears, and to seek Me with all their heart."

My stomach growled loudly, and I was sure the Lord heard it rumbling. "How long do I get to stay here?" A tear trickled down my cheek as I wondered how much time I would have with Mary Grace and Lydia.

"No time at all. You will go back right away."

My heart sank to my tormented stomach, which clenched as I fought the urge to openly sob.

"I will see you again, My son." God spoke softer this

time, His voice still deep and filled with love, but He felt my pain. I was sure of it.

There was no point in arguing, begging to stay. I knew I was going back.

And it happened instantly. I was back in the hospital bed when I opened my eyes, but all was quiet. No monitors beeping, noisy oxygen machine, or doctors scrambling to bring me back to life. Only Amelia. My granddaughter had her back to me as her shoulders shook from crying. I'd been pronounced dead, and presumably, Amelia had been given some time alone with me to grieve.

It occurred to me that I had encountered some sort of near-death experience. Had it all been a dream? I took a deep breath—a deep, full breath like I hadn't taken in years, as if my lungs were that of a healthy twenty-year-old. The aches and pains that consumed most of my body seemed to have fled as I moved slightly in the bed. But it was my knees that spoke to me in an unfamiliar language. They moved and shifted with ease, and I chuckled.

Amelia spun around so fast she backed into a tray filled with medical supplies that went toppling to the floor. As her jaw dropped, my granddaughter looked like she'd seen a ghost before she bolted from the room, screaming for a doctor.

Moments later, three doctors and a nurse came rushing into the room. Amelia stood in the background yelling, "Grandpa, can you hear me? Grandpa?" I'd also been hard of hearing for over a decade.

I waved my arms around so everyone would stop hovering over me and checking my vitals and poking and prodding me. I'd had enough of all that. "Stop! Just stop!" I said with more anger than I had intended. But would all that touching by mere mortals cause my pain to return? I couldn't chance it.

A young doctor, although probably the oldest person in the room, leaned down close to me and said loudly, "Walter, can you hear me?"

"Yes." Frustration fueled the taut strain in my voice. "And there is something I *need*."

"What's that?" The doctor asked, still much too loud for my liking. I glanced back and forth between me and the machine by the bed that was now beeping in a steady rhythm.

"I need a steak, preferably ribeye, medium rare, and a fully loaded baked potato with extra sour cream. A salad would be nice, too, and I'd like blue cheese dressing." I paused, my mouth watering as I envisioned the meal. "And a slice of red velvet cake topped with vanilla ice cream, please."

Amelia was quickly by my side, inching the doctors out of the way. "Grandpa, I love you so much. I thought we'd lost you." She kissed me on the forehead.

I opened my mouth to tell her that she had lost me for a while, but I knew my story would sound crazy.

My granddaughter turned to the doctor and said, "Maybe we should get him some pudding or yogurt or something easy on his stomach."

I growled. "Amelia, I love you. But if someone doesn't round me up a steak, I'm going to rip all these tubes from my arms and get it myself." And I was pretty sure I could.

I regretted my harsh outburst right away, but people started moving quickly after that, checking my vitals and visibly scanning me from head to toe. Amelia promised to take me to my favorite steakhouse, so I practiced patience, which was difficult. My stomach was grumbling, but even more so . . . my life had changed. Something was on the horizon, which felt exhilarating and terrifying at the same time.

THE MESSENGER - CHAPTER 1

Walter savored the taste of his ribeye as his granddaughter gazed at him across the table, her bottom lip trembling slightly. Amelia was likely still in shock. She'd seen her grandfather die, then come back to life like something out of a sci-fi movie.

"I'm not saying that I don't believe you, Grandpa, but you have to admit . . . it's a lot to swallow." Amelia slouched into the booth seat as she folded her hands atop the table. Walter had told her everything as he remembered it.

After he finished the last bite of his steak, he laid his fork across his plate, undecided if he would order that slice of red velvet cake he'd been longing for. "You need to eat something." His granddaughter was too thin. Walter blamed a lot of that on his great-grandson. Michael kept his mother in a continuous state of worry. "And yes . . . I understand that my story is a lot to swallow." He had been questioning the reality of his tale ever since he'd awoken back in his hospital bed. But his lack of pain and bounce

81

in his step was proof that he hadn't imagined the entire thing. He was skeptical about certain recollections though. Walter didn't think he'd ever really met a stranger, often striking up conversations at the grocery store with folks he didn't know, or at the post office, bank, or any public place. But this was different.

He recalled what God had asked him to do. *When you return in the grandest of health, you will meet people who need to hear what I have to say in order to find their way to Me. I will guide you in this endeavor. Just listen for My voice the way you always have.*

How would he deliver—or even recognize—messages he was to convey to people he didn't know? Would the voices in his mind be his own thoughts or speculations? How would he differentiate his thoughts from those coming from God?

As he pondered his situation, he wiped his mouth with his napkin and noticed his lower dentures no longer rubbed the inside of his lip, which made for a much more enjoyable meal. Then he heard sniffling and lifted his eyes to Amelia's just as she dabbed at a tear in the corner of one eye. His granddaughter was forty-three, but right now she reminded him of a young girl. Her bottom lip still trembled, and her face was flushed.

"Doodlebug, what is it?" Walter reached across the table and put a hand on hers. "It's okay if you don't believe me." He eased his hand away and shrugged. "It's hard for me to take in too."

More tears gathered in her beautiful sapphire eyes, just like her grandmother's. "How-how did everyone look? Grandma? Momma? All of them?"

Walter smiled. "Young, healthy, and beautiful."

His Doodlebug—a nickname she'd been given due to her love of the roly-poly bugs when she was little—covered her face with her hands and wept quietly.

"Don't be sad. I know you miss all those who have gone home ahead of us. I do too." Walter recalled how lovely his wife and daughter were in Heaven, and a small dagger pierced his heart as he struggled to recapture the love he'd felt in Mary Grace's arms. Even more so, in the presence of God. "But we will see them again."

Amelia uncovered her face when her phone vibrated on the table. She quickly reached for it but not before Walter saw the name 'Michael' flash across the screen. He gingerly touched his gold-rimmed glasses, which were folded in his shirt pocket and apparently not necessary anymore. He had put the glasses in his pocket when they'd left the hospital, but he hadn't needed them to read the menu.

"Hey," Amelia said softly as she chewed her bottom lip. "Did you get my message about Grandpa?" She waited, and even though Walter had an ear peeled, he couldn't hear his great-grandson's voice. "Yeah, he seems fine."

Walter wondered if Michael's troubles stemmed from not having his father in his life. Amelia and her husband had divorced when Michael was only six, and Trevor rarely saw the boy. At his core, Walter believed the kid to be a good person. A thoughtful young man who had fallen in with the wrong crowd. Walter prayed for the boy constantly. And for his mother, who had never remarried. Amelia's life revolved around her job as an administrative assistant at an oil company and bailing

Michael out of one jam or another. Walter closed his eyes and prayed for a message to give his granddaughter, something to lighten her load, but he didn't hear anything. He wondered if he ever would since that part of his story felt remote. But if anyone needed to give their problems to God, it was Amelia. She was a beautiful woman inside and out, but Walter had never been sure where she stood in her faith. Although today she had given him the impression that she did believe in an after-life when she inquired as to how everyone in Heaven looked.

"Grandpa, I have to go." She sighed before she took a sip of water.

"Is everything okay?" Walter tried to capture her eyes, but she avoided his as she put her phone away. He had his answer.

"I'm sorry to cut things short. Michael . . ." She pressed her mouth closed, then took a deep breath. "I just need to get home. Do you want to get some red velvet cake to go?"

Walter shook his head. "I think I'll just sit here for a spell, let that steak settle, then decide if I want dessert. I'll take a cab home in a bit."

Amelia didn't like it that he took taxis to get around Houston, but when the Department of Public Safety took away his license, he didn't have a choice. He couldn't pass the eye exam. Amelia wasn't always available to drive him around, nor did he want her to have to, so he hailed a cab when he needed a ride. There was a new form of trans-portation called Uber, but he hadn't tried that yet.

A new thought surfaced. He could probably pass the eye exam now, but he'd sold his car over a year ago.

Perhaps he would be in the market for a new vehicle soon and regain some of his independence.

His granddaughter stood and stared at him. "Grandpa . . ." The hint of a smile lit up her face. "I've been talking softly to you, in a normal voice, ever since we left the hospital." She leaned closer and looked at one side of his face.

Walter touched his ears and realized he had forgotten to put his hearing aids in, which wasn't unusual. *Another gift from Heaven.* He gleamed back at her. "And I've heard every word you said. I won't be needing those annoying hearing aids anymore."

"That's amazing." Amelia tipped her head slightly and smiled a little more. "I'm glad today wasn't your day to go."

Walter had longed to stay in Heaven, but he also loved his earthy family, and God had assured him that he would go back someday. "Me too."

She leaned down and kissed him on the forehead. "I'll call you tonight."

Amelia called most nights around six o'clock. She reminded him to take his medicine and to check his calendar for any appointments the following day. Usually, there wasn't anything on the agenda. Maybe a doctor's appointment or an occasional coffee with his old partner at the engineering firm they'd owned and sold twenty years ago.

"I love you, Grandpa," she said before she waved and started toward the exit of the steakhouse.

"I love you, too, Doodlebug."

She moved swiftly and probably didn't hear him. He glanced at the money on the table. Somehow, she always managed to leave money for the meal even though Walter had told her repeatedly that he had plenty of money—enough to last his entire lifetime, which was suddenly in question. How long exactly would that be? Would he have to lose his hearing and sight again? Would all his ailments slowly return? Surely the Lord wouldn't put him through more heart attacks, cancer, and the like. He scratched his chin as he wondered if he would wake up tomorrow morning and realize this had all been a dream.

Then he heard a deep and unmistakable voice in his head. You will know him when you see him, God said in his mind. Not only had this day not been a dream, but Walter had just been given his first message to be delivered to a man outside the restaurant. But Walter didn't move for a few minutes as he wondered if he had heard the message incorrectly. The rest of the message didn't seem to make much sense. *The blue house is not the answer, and neither is Sheila's way. Seek comfort in the house of the Lord.*

Jacob stared at the dirty pavement as he leaned against the outer wall of a restaurant that he could never afford to eat in. At least the owner or one of the staff hadn't come out and asked him to move along like they'd done in the past. He seemed to have the best luck snagging leftovers from people who left the fancy steakhouse, as opposed to fast-food-type places where folks didn't usually have leftovers. Maybe the steakhouse people gave him food because they had plenty of money, or maybe it was because of the way he looked, and they just wanted him to move along.

Most days, his wavy brown hair was dirty and matted from sleeping wherever he could find a place to lay his head. He had two shirts he alternated, and occasionally he got away with rinsing them off in the fountain in front of the bank nearby, although he'd been run off from that spot too.

Never in his life would he have considered dumpster diving for food until three months ago. It was always a last resort, but hunger had a way of pushing a person's limits. Today, he was hoping for a sympathetic soul to offer him some leftovers, something more than a few French fries and part of a burger from a kid's happy meal he'd found atop a trashcan.

He'd spent a lot of time dreaming up legal ways to change his situation, but every option required the one thing he didn't have. Money. It was at the root of everything, evil or not. It bought food to nourish the body, clothed a person, and helped a guy look respectful enough to land a job, which could lead to a roof over his head. Jacob had never stolen anything in his life, but desperation caused him to put it on the agenda for later tonight. He had a plan for this evening, and no one would get hurt. Someday, he'd try to repay whatever he stole.

He looked up every time someone left the restaurant, but only two women exited carrying to-go bags, and they avoided him like the leper he was. It was two in the afternoon. He'd missed the lunch crowd. He wished he could come back closer to dinnertime. People seemed more generous at night. Maybe because they were boozed up and wanted to feel good about themselves. Jacob wasn't sure, but his mouth watered at the thought of leftover steak, chicken, pasta . . . or any other offerings on the menu. But he had just enough money in his pocket to take a cab ride to the blue house later. Then he could buy all the food he wanted.

When it came to people who drank, it seemed to go one way or the other—overly generous or out of control. When his stepfather, Leo, was riding the vodka train, the man didn't feel good about himself and didn't see anything good about Jacob. In Leo's defense, he'd been a decent stepfather until Jacob's mother died. He'd even paid for Jacob to enroll in some online college classes, citing that at twenty-two, it was time to settle on a career, or to at least start thinking about his future. Jacob had mostly held a string of jobs that weren't leading to anything that would classify as a career.

After Jacob's mother died, Leo spiraled into a depression and started knocking Jacob around, blaming him for his mother's death. And he was right. Jacob might as well have slit her wrists himself. He'd certainly driven her to it. He'd been in jail twice for driving drunk, and he'd also been arrested for disorderly conduct. He deserved the life he was living, but he couldn't take it anymore. Jacob would need to either rob the blue house in his old neighborhood where no one was ever home at night, or join his mom in the grave. He was beginning to care less and less about which option won out.

READ THE REST OF *THE MESSENGER ON AMAZON.*

ACKNOWLEDGMENTS

Always a huge Thank You to God for continuing to bless me with stories to tell.

To my husband, Patrick, thanks for loving me AND our fur babies!

Audrey Wick and Janet Murphy, you're both fabulous! Thank you for revising and proofing my manuscripts. They always shine brighter because of your efforts. I'm so grateful and appreciate you both very much.

And, to my readers . . . without you, I wouldn't be able to continue doing what I love while hopefully entertaining you and glorifying God. A BIG THANK YOU!

ABOUT THE AUTHOR

Bestselling and award-winning author Beth Wiseman has sold over 3 million books. She is the recipient of the coveted Holt Medallion, a two-time Carol Award winner, and has won the Inspirational Reader's Choice Award three times. Her books have been on various bestseller lists, including CBD, CBA, ECPA, and *Publishers Weekly*. Beth and her husband are empty nesters enjoying country life in south central Texas.

Made in United States
North Haven, CT
23 June 2024

53960606R00064